W9-AJP-112

Dear Parents:

Congratulations! Your child is taking the first steps on an exciting journey. The destination? Independent reading!

STEP INTO READING® will help your child get there. The program offers five steps to reading success. Each step includes fun stories and colorful art or photographs. In addition to original fiction and books with favorite characters, there are Step into Reading Non-Fiction Readers, Phonics Readers and Boxed Sets, Sticker Readers, and Comic Readers—a complete literacy program with something to interest every child.

Learning to Read, Step by Step!

Ready to Read   Preschool–Kindergarten
• big type and easy words • rhyme and rhythm • picture clues
For children who know the alphabet and are eager to begin reading.

Reading with Help   Preschool–Grade 1
• basic vocabulary • short sentences • simple stories
For children who recognize familiar words and sound out new words with help.

Reading on Your Own   Grades 1–3
• engaging characters • easy-to-follow plots • popular topics
For children who are ready to read on their own.

Reading Paragraphs   Grades 2–3
• challenging vocabulary • short paragraphs • exciting stories
For newly independent readers who read simple sentences with confidence.

Ready for Chapters   Grades 2–4
• chapters • longer paragraphs • full-color art
For children who want to take the plunge into chapter books but still like colorful pictures.

STEP INTO READING® is designed to give every child a successful reading experience. The grade levels are only guides; children will progress through the steps at their own speed, developing confidence in their reading. The F&P Text Level on the back cover serves as another tool to help you choose the right book for your child.

Remember, a lifetime love of reading starts with a single step!

All rights reserved. Published in the United States by Random House Children's Books,
a division of Random House LLC, a Penguin Random House Company, New York.
Originally published in hardcover in the United States by Alfred A. Knopf,
an imprint of Random House Children's Books, New York, in 1969.

Step into Reading, Random House, and the Random House colophon
are registered trademarks of Random House LLC.

Visit us on the Web! StepIntoReading.com   randomhouse.com/kids
Educators and librarians, for a variety of teaching tools, visit us at RHTeachersLibrarians.com

Library of Congress Cataloging-in-Publication Data
Lionni, Leo, 1910–1999, author, illustrator.
Alexander and the wind-up mouse / Leo Lionni.
p. cm. — (Step into reading. Step 3)
"Originally published in hardcover in the United States by Alfred A. Knopf in 1969"—Copyright page.
Caldecott Honor Book, 1970.
Summary: Alexander, a real mouse, wants to be a toy mouse like his friend Willy until he discovers
Willy is to be thrown away.
ISBN 978-0-385-75551-1 (pbk.) — ISBN 978-0-385-75630-3 (lib. bdg.)
[1. Mice—Fiction.] I. Title.
PZ7.L6634Aj 2014 [E]—dc23 2013038785

This book has been officially leveled by using the F&P Text Level Gradient™ Leveling System.

Printed in the United States of America   10 9 8 7 6 5 4 3 2 1

Alexander and the Wind-Up Mouse

by Leo Lionni

Random House New York

"Help! Help! A mouse!"
There was a scream.
Then a crash.
Cups, saucers, and spoons
were flying in all directions.

Alexander ran for his hole
as fast as his little legs
would carry him.

All Alexander wanted
was a few crumbs and yet
every time they saw him
they would scream for help
or chase him with a broom.

One day, when there was no one
in the house, Alexander heard
a squeak in Annie's room.
He sneaked in
and what did he see?
Another mouse.
But not an ordinary mouse
like himself. Instead of legs
it had two little wheels,
and on its back there was a key.

"Who are you?" asked Alexander.

"I am Willy the wind-up mouse,
Annie's favorite toy.
They wind me
to make me run around
in circles, they cuddle me,
and at night I sleep on a soft
white pillow between the doll
and a woolly teddy bear.
Everyone loves me."

"They don't care much for me,"
said Alexander sadly.
But he was happy
to have found a friend.

"Let's go to the kitchen
and look for crumbs," he said.
"Oh, I can't," said Willy.
"I can only move
when they wind me.
But I don't mind.
Everybody loves me."

Alexander, too,
came to love Willy.
He went to visit him
whenever he could.

He told him of his adventures
with brooms, flying saucers,
and mousetraps.
Willy talked about the penguin,
the woolly bear,
and mostly about Annie.
The two friends spent
many happy hours together.

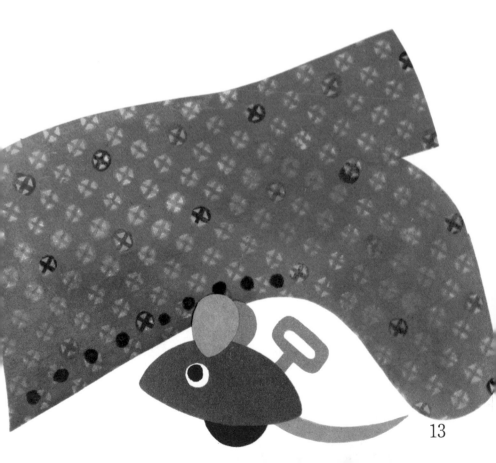

But when he was alone
in the dark of his hideout,
Alexander thought of Willy
with envy.

"Ah!" he sighed.
"Why can't I be
    a wind-up mouse like Willy
    and be cuddled and loved."

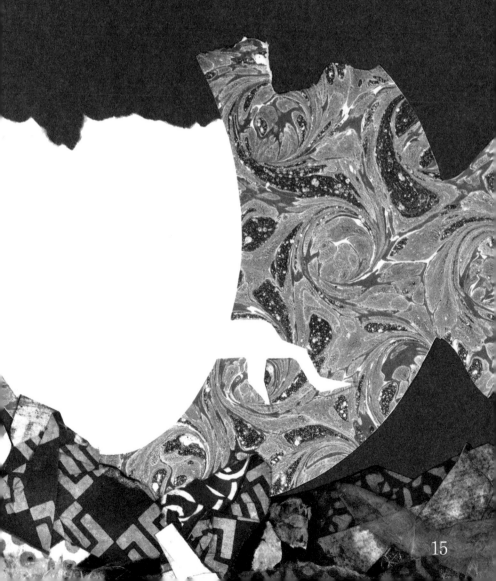

One day
Willy told a strange story.
"I've heard," he whispered
    mysteriously, "that in the garden,
    at the end of the pebblepath,

close to the blackberry bush,
there lives a magic lizard
who can change one animal
into another."
"Do you mean," said Alexander,
"that he could change me
into a wind-up mouse like you?"

That very afternoon
Alexander went into the garden
and ran to the end of the path.
"Lizard, lizard," he whispered.
And suddenly there stood
before him, full of the colors
of flowers and butterflies,
a large lizard. "Is it true that
you could change me into a
wind-up mouse?" asked Alexander
in a quivering voice.

"When the moon is round,"
 said the lizard,
"bring me a purple pebble."

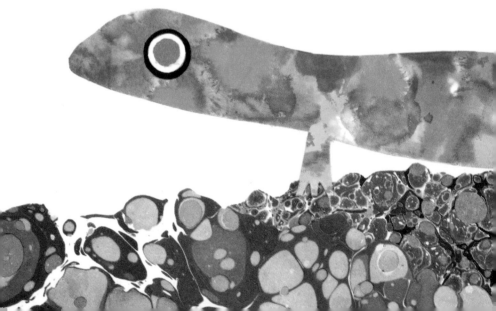

For days and days
Alexander searched
the garden
for a purple pebble.

In vain.
He found yellow pebbles
and blue pebbles
and green pebbles—
but not one
tiny purple pebble.

At last, tired and hungry,
he returned to the house.
In a corner of the pantry
he saw a box full of old toys,
and there, between blocks
and broken dolls, was Willy.
"What happened?"
said Alexander, surprised.

Willy told him a sad story.
It had been Annie's birthday.
There had been a party and
everyone had brought a gift.

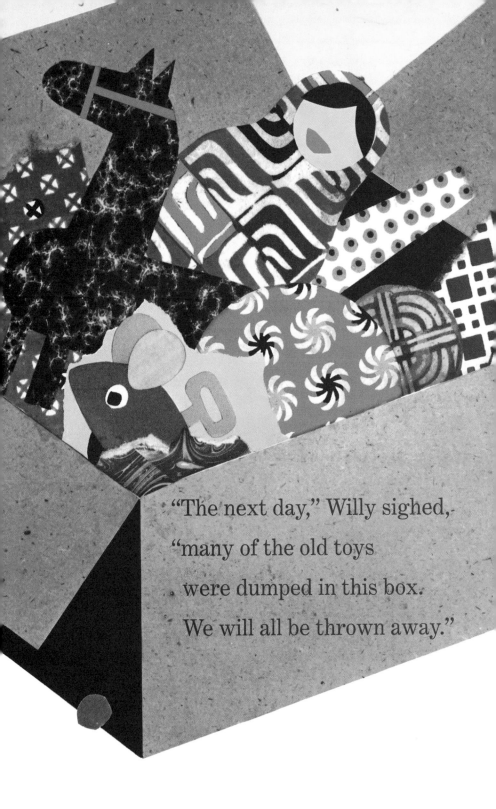

"The next day," Willy sighed,
"many of the old toys
were dumped in this box.
We will all be thrown away."

Alexander was almost
in tears. "Poor, poor Willy!"
he thought. But then suddenly
something caught his eye.
Could it really be...?
Yes it was!
It was a little purple pebble.

All excited, he ran
to the garden, the precious
pebble tight in his arms.
There was a full moon.
Out of breath, Alexander stopped
near the blackberry bush.
"Lizard, lizard, in the bush,"
he called quickly.

The leaves rustled
and there stood the lizard.

"The moon is round, the pebble
found," said the lizard.
"Who or what do you wish to be?"
"I want to be . . ."
Alexander stopped.
Then suddenly he said,
"Lizard, lizard, could you change
Willy into a mouse like me?"

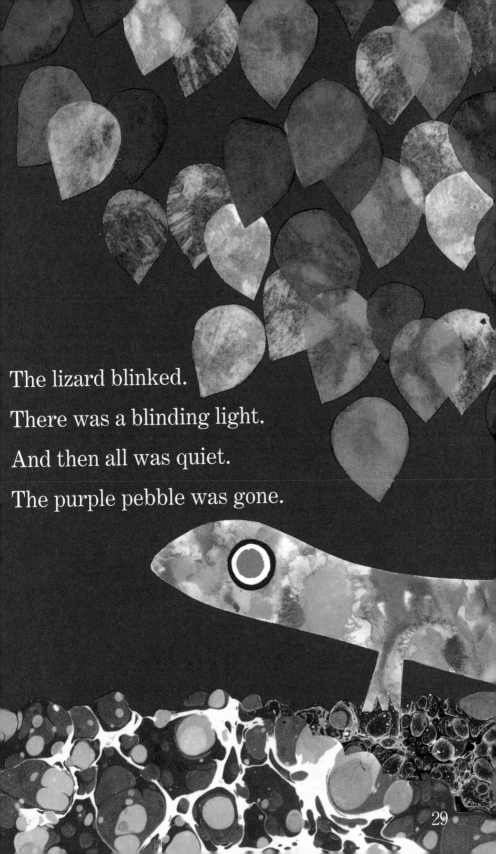

The lizard blinked.

There was a blinding light.

And then all was quiet.

The purple pebble was gone.

Alexander ran
back to the house
as fast as he could.

The box was there,
but alas it was empty.
"Too late," he thought,
and with a heavy heart
he went to his hole
in the baseboard.

Something squeaked!
Cautiously Alexander
moved closer to the hole.
There was a mouse inside.
"Who are you?" said Alexander,
a little frightened.

"My name is Willy,"
said the mouse.

"Willy!" cried Alexander.
"The lizard . . . the lizard did it!"
  He hugged Willy
  and then they ran
  to the garden path.
  And there they danced
  until dawn.

LEO LIONNI wrote and illustrated more than forty picture books in his lifetime, including four Caldecott Honor Books—*Inch by Inch, Swimmy, Frederick,* and *Alexander and the Wind-Up Mouse.* He died in 1999 at the age of 89.

Praise for Leo Lionni

"If the picture book is a new visual art form in our time, Leo Lionni is certain to be judged a master of the genre."

—Selma Lanes, *The New York Times*

Frederick the field mouse won't collect food for the coming winter. Will he still be able to help his fellow mice in the cold days ahead?

STEP INTO READING®

3
STEP
READING ON YOUR OWN

Frederick
by Leo Lionni